THE MOPWATER FILES

THE MOPWATER FILES

John R. Erickson

Illustrations by Gerald L. Holmes

Maverick Books
Published by Gulf Publishing Company
Houston, Texas

Copyright © 1997 by John R. Erickson. All rights, including
reproduction by photographic or electronic process and
translation into other languages, are fully reserved under the
International Copyright Union, the Universal Copyright
Convention, and the Pan-American Copyright Convention.
Reproduction or use of this book in whole or in part in any
manner without written permission of the publisher is strictly
forbidden.

Maverick Books
Published by Gulf Publishing Company
P. O. Box 2608, Houston, Texas 77252-2608

10   9   8   7   6   5   4   3   2   1

Library of Congress Cataloging-in-Publication Data

Erickson, John R., 1943–
   The mopwater files / John R. Erickson ; illustrations by
Gerald L. Holmes.
      p.   cm. — (Hank the Cowdog ; 28)
   Summary: Hank the Cowdog, head of ranch security,
discovers that drinking a bucket of plant food restores his
energy, leading to a series of embarrassing near-disasters.
   ISBN 0-87719-313-4 (pbk.). — **ISBN 0-87719-314-2** (hc)
   1. Dogs—Fiction.   [1. Dogs—Fiction.   2. West (U.S.)—
Fiction.   3. Humorous stories.]   I. Holmes, Gerald L., ill.   II.
Title.   III. Series: Erickson, John R., 1943–   Hank the
Cowdog ; 28.
PS3555.R428M665   1997
813′.54—dc21   96-49464
                                                        CIP
                                                        AC

Printed in the United States of America.
Hank the Cowdog is a registered trademark of John R. Erickson.

To Kit and Geraldine

C O N T E N T S

C H A P T E R

1

TOTAL MELTDOWN
ON THE RANCH

It's me again, Hank the Cowdog. Have we ever discussed the Mopwater Files? Maybe not, because it's still Highly Classified information and we're not ready to go public with it.

We may never go public with it. It's too secret. Oh, and it has a scary ending. You wouldn't like it.

That's too bad. It was a pretty interesting case but I'm just not in a position to . . .

Do you remember Rufus the Doberman pinscher? Big guy, little green eyes, sharp-pointed ears, long fangish teeth. A terrible bully, always tormenting Miss Beulah the Collie, and you talk about ugly! He was ugly, inside and out.

It's still hard to believe that I actually challenged that guy to a fight to the death, but then came the bucket of toxic mopwater and . . .

Oops. I wasn't supposed to reveal anything about the case. Forget I said anything. Why, if this information fell into the wrong hands . . . just forget it. That's all I can say.

What were we talking about? Oh yes, the weather. It was the middle of the summer, see, and hotter than blue blazes. It had been hot for days and weeks, and there I was, wearing a fur coat.

Yellowjacket wasps hummed in the still air and you could see heat waves shimmering on the horizon. The wind had quit blowing. The windmills had quit pumping. The cowboys had quit working.

I had started out the morning in a nice piece of shade beneath the gas tanks, but by eleven o'clock the shade had . . . I don't know what happened to it. It had burned up or boiled away or something, and I found myself lying in the scorching glare of the sun.

What a cheap trick! I had to summon up huge reserves of energy to move myself to another piece of shade on the west side of the storage tank. It was tough, let me tell you, and I just barely made it.

But you know what? Something happened to that shade too, and within an hour I was roasting again. And all at once I faced the toughest decision of the day: Would I get up and move my freight to

G.L.Holmes

another shady spot, or would I just lie there and roast?

I raised my head and studied the situation. I could see the shade. There it was, not more than six inches from my present location, but to get there, I would have to go through the entire Jack

Up and Move procedure, just as though I were moving halfway across the ranch.

That doesn't seem fair, does it? If a guy travels no more than a few inches, he shouldn't have to go to all that trouble. Think about it. Raise head. Position legs under body. Push up on front legs. Push up on back legs. Coordinate the Walking Pattern for all four feet. Walk six inches to the west. Collapse.

It wasn't fair. It was an outrage, and I decided that I wouldn't do it. By George, I would just lie there in the sun and roast. That would teach them . . . whoever They were . . . and I hoped They would take notice and quit messing around with my shade.

I laid my head down and began roasting. I heard my deep breathing and listened to the stupid flies buzzing around my ears. I hate 'em. If I'd had more energy, I would have raised up and snapped 'em all out of the air.

Snapped 'em out of the air and chewed 'em up into little bitty pieces of legs and wings, and then spit 'em all out on the ground. That's what a fly deserves and that was how much I hated the little tormenting devils, but I didn't have the energy to initiate a good Anti-fly Defense Program.

So I just lay there in the sun and roasted, and let the flies walk around my ears . . . over my face . . .

Into my nose?

Okay, that did it. They could have the ears but no fly walks into my nose. I lifted my head and cut loose a withering barrage of snapping. I missed them all, but they got the message and left my nose alone.

And, what the heck, once I had gone to all the trouble to raise my head, I figured I might as well go on into Jack Up and Move. I jacked myself up, staggered five steps to the west, and collapsed.

Whew! I was exhausted, but at least I wasn't roasting. I closed my eyes and tried to sleep. That's what I needed. Sleep. About two weeks of solid sleep.

Unfortunately, Slim the Cowboy came along just then. I cracked one eye but didn't lift my head. Too exhausted. Slim was a pretty good fellow, but not so good that I could afford to squander a lot of energy saying hello. Not in this heat.

He stopped in the same piece of shade that I was occupying. He pulled a bandanna out of his hip pocket and mopped his face.

"Boy, it's hot. The weather report's prescribing another day over a hundred. This'll make about five days in a row."

Yes, I was aware of that.

"It kind of saps a guy of energy, don't it, Hankie?"

Right.

"And you're just going to lay there in the shade, aren't you?"

Yep.

"You're not even going to jump up and wag your tail and tell me how wonderful I am, are you?"

Nope.

"It kind of hurts my feelings, Hankie."

Life is hard.

"Well, I wish I could just lay around in the shade, but some of us have to work for a living."

That was a cheap shot. For his information, I not only had a job but a very important job. It just happened that . . . well, I had run out of energy and ambition.

You won't believe this. He flopped down on the gravel drive and pillowed his head on my rib cage. Had I invited him to . . . urg . . . put his sweaty head in the middle of my poor exhausted body? No. I considered taking countermeasures but . . . too much trouble.

"Ahhh! That's better, but you're awful boney for a pillow."

Well, if he didn't like my bones, he could go find a jellyfish. And speaking of bones, his head wasn't any featherbed. It was solid bone and it was heavy and hot and I didn't need it on my rib cage, thank you.

"Boy, this heat is terrible. It didn't used to bother me, but it sure does now. I've got thirty-seven jobs to do and enough energy for about three of 'em."

Me too.

"Too many birthdays, Hank. Don't you reckon that's the main problem?"

I had no opinion on that.

At last he raised up to a sitting position. He looked down at me and grinned. I summoned up the energy to whap my tail on the ground three times. Whew!

"Well, this has been fun, Hankie, but I'd better go pack them wheel bearings on the stock trailer. I can already tell that you ain't going to do it."

Correcto.

With much grunting and muttering, he pushed himself up and shuffled off to the machine shed.

At last, peace and quiet. I closed my eyes and began floating out on the sea of snork morkus skittlebomb . . .

Huh? My eyes popped open. Someone had moved my shade again! Was this some kind of joke? What was the deal? Every time I got comfortable, some idiot . . .

I summoned my last reserves of energy and . . . Drover? There he was in front of me, giving me his usual foolish grin.

"Hi Hank. What you doing?"

"What I'm doing is trying to sleep, Drover, and restore my precious bodily fluids, but some maniac keeps moving my shade around. Did you see anybody messing with my shade?"

"Well, let me think here. I saw Slim."

"No, it wasn't him. I had him under constant surveillance."

"Boy, that's a big word."

"Thanks."

"I wonder what it means."

I dragged myself back into the shade and flopped down. "I don't know what it means. I don't have the energy to explain it. I'm sorry I brought it up."

"Oh, that's okay. Sure is hot, isn't it?"

I glared ice picks at him. "Yes it is, Drover, so why are you so chirpy?"

"Oh, I don't know. I've been watching the chickens chase grasshoppers."

"Great."

"You ever watch a chicken chase a grasshopper?"

"Yes."

"It's kind of neat, isn't it?"

"No."

"I mean, they're pretty good at it."

"It's their business, Drover. If you're a chicken, that's what you do. Good night."

"Good night . . . only it's the middle of the day."

"I'm aware of that."

"Boy, it sure is hot."

"That's why I'm shaded up, Drover. It's too hot to do any work, so snorkle the mirking piffle."

"Yeah, but I can't sleep and I get bored. You ever get bored?"

"Snork."

"I do. You ever try to catch a grasshopper?"

"No."

"Me neither, but I bet I could. Want me to try?"

"Sure. Go catch a pifflehopper."

"Okay, here I go."

At last! Peace and quiet. I sank into the warm embrace of a delicious dream and . . . Beulah? My goodness, there she was in all her splintering glory: the deep brown eyes, the flaxen hair, the perfect collie nose, the smile that said . . .

C H A P T E R

2

DROVER EATS A GRASSHOPPER

"**I** caught one, Hank!"

I lifted my head and opened both eyes and looked at the front in face of me. "Beulah?"

"No, a grasshopper."

"What are you and who are you doing where?"

"Well, let's see. My name's Drover and I'm your best friend and I just caught a grasshopper."

"Just because you're a grasshopper doesn't mean you're a friend of mine. Where am I?" I blinked my eyes. "Okay, it's coming back now. You're Drover."

"That's what I said."

"There for a second, I thought you were Beulah."

"No, it must have been me, 'cause I'm all I've ever been."

I stared at the runt. "What?"

11

"I said, I'm all I've ever been but I caught a grasshopper."

"That doesn't make a lick of sense." All at once, he licked his chops. "Will you stop that?"

"Stop what?"

"I've told you over and over not to do that."

"What did I do?"

"I said that you're not making a lick of sense and . . ." He licked his chops again! "There, you see? You keep doing it. What's wrong with you?"

"Well, I can't help it."

I hoisted myself up to a sitting position and turned a withering glare on my . . . whatever he was. My nitwit assistant, I guess.

"Of course you can help it. It's a totally absurd and meaningless gesture."

"Not really. See, I ate a grasshopper and that's why I was licking my chops."

"You ATE a grasshopper?"

"Yep, I sure did. Caught him with my own two paws and ate him with my own mouth."

I gave my head a shake. "Drover, that's disgusting. Eating a grasshopper? Son, chickens eat grasshoppers, but dogs don't."

"Yeah, but I did."

"That's appalling."

"No, it was appealing."

"Don't correct my spelling and don't try to put words into my mouth. I said it was appalling and that's exactly what I meant."

"Yeah, but I ate the grasshopper and you didn't, so maybe you don't know how it tasted."

I narrowed my eyes at him. "I can't believe you said that. Have you no respect for your elders, your betters, your superiors? Just because I've never eaten a grasshopper, you think I don't know how they taste?"

"Well, that makes sense to me."

"I'm shocked, Drover, shocked and dismayed and disappointed that you would . . . okay, just for the sake of argument, how did it taste?"

He grinned. "Well . . . it was pretty good."

"See? I gave you a chance to express yourself and what did you do?"

"Well . . . I told the truth."

"No, you didn't tell the truth. You contradicted my Theory on Grasshoppers, is what you did, and if you can't give the right answer, what good is freedom of speech?"

"Well, I don't know. But I ate a grasshopper and it was pretty good. And you ought to try one yourself."

I curled my lip. "I will never eat a grasshopper. Bird dogs will fly before I eat a grasshopper. Hogs will ride sidesaddles before I eat a grasshopper."

"They're better than you think."

"No sale, Drover."

"And they're better than dry dog food."

"I don't want to hear it."

"They taste kind of like chicken."

"Well, of course they do, because that's what chickens eat."

"Yeah, and you like the taste of chicken, don't you?"

"No, I . . ." All at once it appeared that my mouth was watering, as I, uh, recalled several delicious ultra-secret chicken dinners I had . . .

I licked my chops, so to speak, and was unable to answer the question.

Drover grinned. "See? I said 'chicken' and you licked your chops, and that's proof that you like chicken."

"I did not lick my chops, and even if I had, it would prove almost nothing, for you see, Drover, ranch dogs are forbidden to eat . . . slurp . . . chickens—for good and obvious reasons."

"Yeah, but that's my point."

I gave him a hard glare. "Your point? Who or whom do you think you are, and when did you

start putting points into your pointless con-
versations?"

"Well, I don't know, but I've got one now. You
want to hear it?"

I heaved a sigh. "Okay, let's hear it."

His grin faded. "Gosh, I just lost it. I can't remember. Oh darn."

"Will you hurry up? I'm a very busy dog."

"Okay, here we go, I've got it. The point is that
grasshoppers taste like chicken, so when you eat
a grasshopper, it's almost like eating a chicken."

I licked my chops. "Hmmm. Not a bad point,
actually. And you know, Sally May hates grasshoppers."

"Yeah, 'cause they eat up her garden."

"Exactly. So we're looking at possible bonus
points here. Hmmm." I ran that one through my
data banks. "I find only one major flaw in your oint-
ment, Drover. The back legs of a grasshopper are
known to have spurs or barbs, which might lodge
in the throats of certain dogs."

He grinned and shrugged. "Well, they didn't
bother me. I guess you have to chew 'em up, is all."

"Hmmm, yes. But we still have one problem,
Drover. I don't have the energy to catch a grasshopper. It's this heat. It drains me of all energy and
ambition. I don't want to do anything but sleep.
It's very discouraging."

15

"Well, maybe a couple of fresh grasshoppers would help. They always seem to have plenty of energy, and so do the chickens."

"Hmmm." I heaved a sigh and pushed myself up on all fours. "Okay, Drover, I'll give it a shot. But if this doesn't work, I'll have to put it in your record."

We made our way down to the yard gate. I happened to know that Sally May was out working in her yard, for I had seen her there before my nap . . . that is, before I had checked into the shade for, uh, treatment of extreme exhaustion and loss of precious bodily fluids.

I knew she was out there, working and slaving in the heat of the day, in a heroic effort to beautify her house and therefore the ranch itself. I admired her dedication to greenery and beauty and so forth, and would have done almost anything to help her out.

You'll notice that Slim and Loper were nowhere in sight. Bring out a shovel or a rake and those guys disappear. It's like showing a cross to an umpire.

They vanish like dewdrops in August.

But there was Sally May, working and slaving in the hot sun; digging holes and planting tender little shrubberies and flowers around the yard fence. And what was the mainest threat to her tender little shrubberies and flowers and plants?

16

Grasshoppers.

You work and slave to put out your stuff, and the minute you walk away, the grasshoppers move in and start mowing 'em down. They're a plague, a pestilence, a minutes to society, and they've been known to break the heart of many a courageous ranch wife.

As Head of Ranch Security, I considered it my duty—nay, my privilege—to rush to the defense

of my master's wife and to protect her yard and greenery from all villains, monsters, and pests.

And especially the hated grasshoppers.

I was the first to arrive on the scene. I did a quick visual sweep and . . . hmmm, there was her cat lurking nearby. When our eyes met, he arched his back and hissed.

Why? It had nothing to do with fear. Pete wasn't smart enough to be afraid of a dog. No, he hissed out of sheer spite and jealousy. See, he thinks he's Sally May's precious kitty and he can't stand the thought of sharing her attention with anyone else.

So he hissed at me. Perhaps he thought this would throw me into an inflammation; that I would bark and give him the pounding he deserved, and that Sally May would rush to his defense.

He thought, in other words, that he could use a cheap cat trick to get me in trouble with the lady of the house, but Pete had used that trick too often in the past and it happened that I was prepared for it.

Hencely, instead of barking and causing a scene, I gave him a, shall we say, toothy smile. I thought that would be the end of it. I was wrong. It turned out to be just the beginning.

3

I'M FORCED TO HUMBLE THE CAT

"Hi Kitty. It's so nice to see you again."

"I don't think you mean that, Hankie."

"Of course I mean it. A day without a cat is like a picnic without flies—imperfect and incomplete."

"Very funny, Hankie, but I think you'd better move along. I'm helping Sally May plant flowers and we don't need you blundering around."

Drover had joined me by then and I turned to him. "Hey Drover, did you hear that?"

"Hear what?"

"Pete just informed me that he's *helping* Sally May."

"I'll be derned. What a nice kitty."

"You missed the point, Drover. It was a stupid statement and a typical cat lie. Cats never help anyone but themselves."

"Oh yeah. Boy, what a stapid stutement."

"Exactly. Have you ever heard a stapider stutement in your life?"

"Well . . . what's a stutement?"

I heaved a sigh. "Drover, please. I'm trying to build my case against this cat. It's very simple. It's very easy. All you have to do is give the correct answer, which is no."

"No."

"Oh, so now you're refusing to obey orders, is that right? I've been noticing this little rebellious streak in you, Drover, and I can tell you that it's going to cause you nothing but trouble."

"I just gave you the right answer, that's all. You said the answer was no and I said no."

"Oh. Well, perhaps . . ." I whirled around and faced the cat. He had moved. I marched over to him. "There, you see, Pete? An impartial panel of two dogs agrees that your studer was stapled and . . ." Suddenly I had lost the thread of my argument. I whirled back to Drover. "Drover, what was the point we were trying to make?"

"Gosh, I don't know. I'm all confused. Something about grasshoppers, I think."

"Yes, of course." I whirled back to the cat. "You see, Kitty, if you were really and truly trying to help Sally May with her planting chores, you would be catching grasshoppers."

The cat stared at me with those weird eyes of his. "Oh really? Why would I be catching grasshoppers?"

"Because, Kitty, grasshoppers are the sworn enemies of every ranch wife, because grasshoppers eat plants and flowers and shrubberies."

"How interesting! The only problem, Hankie, is that grasshoppers can make you choke—the back legs, you know. They hang up in your throat sometimes." Drover and I exchanged glances. Then we started laughing.

"Hey Drover, did you hear that?"

"Yeah, hee hee. I can't believe he said that. What a stapid stutement. He doesn't know that we eat grasshoppers all the time, does he?"

I whirled back to the cat. "For your information, Kitty, we eat grasshoppers all the time. Not only do we rid the ranch of these miserable pests, but we also increase our intake of protein and save the ranch money on dog food. And do we look choked, Pete? Are we coughing and gasping for breath? Ha! So much for your phony argument."

Drover was jumping up and down. "Nice shot, Hank, nice shot! Boy, you really got him on that one."

"Thanks, Drover, but I'm just getting warmed over." I leaned forward and put my nose in Kitty's face. "Your problem with grasshoppers, Pete, is that you're too fat and lazy to catch one."

Pete grinned and rolled his eyes. "Oh really? And I suppose you're going to show me how it's done, hmmm?"

I gave Drover a wink. "He just stepped into our trap, Drover."

"Yeah, boy, we've got him now!"

Back to the cat. "Yes, as a matter of fact, Kitty, that's exactly what we're fixing to do. Before your very eyes, we will put on a live demonstration of Doggie Pest Control. Pay attention and study your lessons."

He grinned and widened his eyes. "Oh, I will, I will. I can hardly wait to see this."

I turned to Drover. "Okay, pal, which one of us will lead off?"

"Oh, I guess I could, since I know more about it than you do."

There was a moment of silence. "I can't believe you said that, Drover."

"Well, I . . ."

"See, you've done it but I've *studied* it. I've studied it from all angles, the ups and the downs and the sidewayses of it."

"Yeah but . . ."

"You may know a little more about the simple act of catching grasshoppers, but I'm much further advanced in the theoretical aspects of pest control."

"I'll be derned."

"See, you've got to have a plan and a theory, Drover. You can't just go out and pounce on a grasshopper."

"Boy, it sure is complicated."

I placed a paw on his shoulder. "It is, and I'm afraid I'll have to handle this one myself. Work a little harder on the theoretical side and maybe next time we'll let you go first."

With that, I went into my warm-up procedures and began loosening up the enormous muscles in my shoulders. Those big muscles up front are the ones you use in these situations—the *jumpus* muscle and the *semi-lateral boogaloo,* if you want to get into the scientific names.

Anyways, I got 'em warmed up and ready for combat. Then I tossed a glance over at Sally May. She was on her knees, digging in the dirt with a hand trowel. Beside her, several feet away, was a bucket of . . . something.

Water, it appeared, yes, it was water because she poured some of it around the roots of the plant she was planting.

Well, she seemed deeply involved in her planting business and hadn't noticed me, so I went over to, well, wish her a good morning and to alert her to the fact that something important was fixing to happen.

I approached her with a big cowdog smile and Broad Swings of the tail. It was lousy luck that I stepped on one of her . . . posies, pansies, petunias, whatever they were . . . stepped on one of her flowers.

And, okay, maybe one of my Broad Swings went a little wild and knocked over a potted plant . . . two potted plants . . . several potted plants, and more or less whipped the straw hat off her head.

Boy, you sure have to watch those Broad Swings of the tail. Sometimes they're so full of joy and emotion, they get out of control and . . .

My goodness, she whirled on me with flared nostrils and flaming eyes. "Will you take your washtub feet and whiplash tail and GET AWAY FROM ME!!!"

Well, sure. I mean, I was just trying to . . . hey, I could take a hint, and yes, I moved away from her.

Sally May can be a little strange sometimes.

But the important thing was that I had made her aware of my presence on the scene, and now I was ready to begin the Pest Control Procedure.

I wanted her to see the whole thing. I knew she would be proud. And I knew she would regret the hateful things she had said.

I didn't have "washtub feet" and I sure hadn't given her "whiplash" with my tail.

Those were Broad Swings of the tail, and they're meant to show friendship and caring and love and devotion.

Sometimes you can't avoid misunderstanding, no matter how hard you try.

A big heart is no match for a small mind . . . although I would be the last to suggest that Sally May had . . . better quit while I'm ahead.

Well, it was Show Time. Everyone was watching me—Pete, Drover, Sally . . . okay, maybe she wasn't exactly watching me, but I was confident that I would grab her attention when the action started.

And you know who else showed up? J.T. Cluck, the Head Rooster. Say, this event was really drawing a crowd, which didn't exactly break my heart. I must confess that I kind of enjoy showing my stuff to an audience, and the bigger the audience the better the performance.

J.T. peered at me and twisted his head around. "What's a-going on around here?"

"Stand back, J.T. I'm fixing to give a public demonstration of Grasshopper Capturation."

"What's that mean?"

"It means that if you will get your feathers out of the way, I will demonstrate the theory and technique of capturing grasshoppers."

"Huh! What does a dog know about catchin' grasshoppers? If you want to know about grasshoppers, talk to a rooster. That's what we do for a living, is what we do."

"Would you move?"

"Huh? Of course they move. They don't just sit there. They hop. That's why they're called grasshoppers. And I'll tell you something else, pooch. They're hard to swaller. You know them back legs? They scrape all the way down and if you ain't real careful, you'll choke, is what'll happen."

"Thank you, J.T. Now, if you'll just . . ."

"Happened to Elsa's brother's uncle. What was his name? Oh yeah, they called him Red. He was red, see, the reddest darn rooster you ever saw. Had green tail feathers."

"J.T."

"Choked on a grasshopper one day is what he done, and died."

I stuck my nose in his face and rattled his beak with a ferocious bark. "MOVE!"

Heh, heh. That got his attention. He jumped three feet into the air, flapped and squawked, and left several feathers floating in the breeze. And best of all, he shut his beak and moved out of the way.

Never argue with a rooster, I always say. Just go straight to the bottom line and give 'em a blast.

At last I was ready.

C H A P T E R

4

GRASSHOPPERS TASTE YUCKO

I did a Visual and Sniffatory Scan of the gravel drive. My instruments zeroed in on a target, bearing 197 degrees and 5.773 megawatts west of the yard gate. It was a smallish green hopper, of the Omega Class.

I shifted into Stealthy Crouch Mode and . . .

"There's a nice little one over there, Hank. See him? You probably ought to start with a little one."

That was Drover. His voice not only broke my concentration but it also alerted the grasshopper to my approach. He hopped away. The grasshopper, that is, not Drover.

I marched over to him. To Drover, that is, not the grasshopper. "Drover, hush."

"I was just trying to help."

"I know you were trying to help, but don't. Just watch and learn and prepare yourself for the day when you too can catch grasshoppers."

He gave me an empty stare. "I thought I knew how. I thought you were the one . . . boy, I'm all confused." Suddenly his eyes grew wide. "Oh my gosh, there's a huge one!"

My laser-like gaze swung around and fixated on the alleged "huge one." By George, he *was* huge (of the Alfalfa Beta Big Boy Class, if you're familiar with the military terminology). He was one of those big green hoppers that can't fly and don't even hop very well because they're so fat.

Not only are they an easy mark, but they're also rich in protein, vitamins, minerals, and rigmaroles. In other words, they're the very best kind for restoring youth and energy.

Speaking of which, I was running low. I could feel my precious reserves of energy ebbing away. I had to hurry.

"This could be the one, Drover."

"Well . . . I don't know. He's awful big."

I gave him a worldly smile. "So am I, Drover. Watch this."

And with that, I switched all scanning devices over to automatic and shifted into Attack Mode. For those of you interested in the technical

aspects, I made this approach at three knots, with ears at three-quarters alert and a stiffened tail at 22 degrees.

That sounds pretty complicated, doesn't it? A lot of dogs wouldn't have gone to so much trouble for a mere grasshopper. I mean, they would have just slopped and slouched in there, but I take pride in my work. No job is too small to be little, is the way I look at it.

And besides, this was no ordinary grasshopper. His Hopping Molecules were going to restore my youthful vigor.

I crept forward on paws that made not a sound—nose out, tail out, and ears up. The audience was silent. Every eye was locked on the unfolding drama. I could almost feel the tension. Then . . . a voice. Sally May's voice.

"What on earth is that dog doing now?"

Good. She was watching. I hoped she would realize that I was doing this to save her precious tender shrubberies and flowers from the Grasshopper Plague.

Yes, we'd had our ups and downs, Sally May and I, and more than our share of misunderstandings. But perhaps this selfless act of selfless devotion would make up for whatever tiny mistakes I'd made in the past.

I crept towards the target on paws that made . . . I've already said that. Five feet away from Ground Zero, I halted, shifted my weight to a point directly over my powerful hind legs, went into a 75% crouch, tensed every muscle in my body, and took a deep breath of . . . well, air of course.

I cast one last glance towards the audience. Not a single eye blinked. I had their total concentration. And yes, even Sally May was watching.

My gaze swung back to the target. It was time. All my years of study and training had come down to this one moment. I dared not fail.

Suddenly I exploded outward and upward—like a rocket, an artillery shell, an arrow seeking its target. My front paws landed first, as you might have guessed, and trapped the hateful grasshopper villain. I could feel him kicking and trying to escape, but there was no chance of that.

I heard Drover cheering me on. "You got 'im, Hank! Nice shot, way to go!"

I lifted my left paw and there he was, a huge, green, hateful, yard-eating grasshopper. "This one's for Sally May!" I yelled, and swept him up in my powerful jaws.

Crunch. Crunch. Gulp. Yes! The deed was done.

I turned and faced the audience. Drover was jumping up and down. Pete wore a sour smile. J.T. had his head twisted, as though he hadn't really figured out what had happened.

And Sally May . . . her eyes were shining in purest admiration and I heard her exclaim, "Did he just eat a grasshopper?"

Heh heh. You bet, and I'd done it all just for
. . . that grasshopper didn't taste much like
chicken to me, and the longer the taste lin-
gered in my mouth, the lesser it reminded me
of chicken . . . or anything else I'd ever wanted
to eat.

To tell the truth, it reminded me of . . . yucko!
. . . green slime and old chewing tobacco and
brussels sprout juice and . . .

I lifted my lips and moved my tongue around,
in hopes of cleansing my mouth of . . . THAT
THING TASTED HORRIBLE! What did grasshoppers eat to give themselves such a wretched . . .
garbage, rotten stinking garbage, that's what they
ate, and what kind of moron would think that
this was the taste of CHICKEN?

Oh, what a fool I'd been, to believe anything that
Drover . . . I swallowed extra hard to get the awful
green garbage taste out of my . . . GULK, WHEEZE,
ARG . . . mouth, but now it appeared that something had lodged in my . . . HARK, HACK, HONK
. . . throat.

And fellers, all at once I could neither swallow
nor draw a breath of . . . I pawed at my mouth. No
luck there. I opened my mouth and fluttered my
tongue around.

Holy smokes, my oxygen supply was running low! I leaped into the air. I ran in a circle, using up the last of my energy supply.

I could hear my body making incredible sounds as it fought to rid itself of . . . whatever it was . . . grasshopper legs, no doubt, with their barbs and spurs, and I had known all along . . . I had told Drover . . .

Water! I had to find some water! My desperate eyes fell upon the red bucket that Sally May had been using. I lurched over to it, stuck my head inside, and began lapping water with all my heart and soul.

Ah-h-h-h! Sweet relief! The lump of poisonous grasshopper legs passed on down my whatever-you-call-it, the pipe that goes from your mouth to your stomach, and I hoped the old stomach was ready for what was about to hit.

The Grasshopper Ordeal had left me exhausted. That was bad news, for it pretty muchly destroyed Drover's nitwit theory that grasshoppers were full of minerals and vitamins.

I sank down to the ground. I had squandered the last of my energy reserves on this deal, and now I was wiped out.

I turned my watering eyes toward my master's wife, wagged my tail, and gave her a weak smile. I hoped she would be . . . burp . . . proud.

She appeared to be . . . well . . . laughing, so to speak, which struck me as slightly inappropriate, seeing as how I had come within one grasshopper leg of choking to death.

I mean, maybe that was no big deal to her but . . . by George, she was getting quite a chuckle out of my moment on death's doormat.

But why all the laughter? I had never supposed that Sally May was the kind of woman who laughed at the misfortunes of others, and yet . . .

She was sitting on the ground, with her arms draped around her knees. At last she gained control of her laughter. "Hank, do you know what you just drank?"

Well . . . uh . . . water?

"That isn't water. It's ROOT STIMULATOR."

Huh?

Root stimulator?

She was biting back a smile. "It's plant food and I don't think it'll hurt you, but maybe you'd better stay out of it." She laughed and shook her head and returned to her planting chores.

For crying out loud, had I escaped one form of poisoning only to fall victim to another? Actually, the stuff had tasted pretty good.

At that very moment, Little Alfred stuck his head out the door. "Hey Mom, Molly's awake fwom her nap and she's twying to get out of her cwib."

"Oh dear." Sally May jumped to her feet and brushed off her hands and pants. "Well, that's the end of the planting for today." She cut her eyes in my direction. "Don't drink that stuff, Hank. It's good for flowers but it might not be good for dumb dogs."

Yes ma'am.

I watched as she loped to the house. And, yes, I tried to forgive her for that last cutting remark— something about "dumb dogs." That was my reward, it seemed, for ridding her yard of . . . burp . . . that grasshopper taste was still in my mouth.

I would never eat another stupid grasshopper. Never.

The back door slammed. She was gone, but the green garbage taste remained in my mouth. My eyes drifted to the, uh, red bucket, so to speak.

You know, I'd never tasted anything quite like that stuff. It had a kind of fizz that tickled a guy's tongue and mouth, and just a hint of a sour taste, and as I sat there . . .

For no particular reason, my mouth began to water and my tongue shot out several times and . . . hmmm . . . by George, much to my own surprise, I found myself . . .

C H A P T E R

5

MY TREMENDOUS SCIENTIFIC DISCOVERY

Lap, lap, lap.

I couldn't see that it would harm anyone or anything if I sampled it one more time. I mean, she'd said it wasn't poison, right? And that little fizzy sour taste sure had covered up the . . .

Lap, lap.

Yes, it definitely helped get the gooey grasshopper taste out of my . . . but you know what? All at once I became aware of something else, something truly remarkable.

I felt a rush of energy!

It was small at first, as the tingle in my mouth moved out to other portions of my exhausted body. It tickled my nose, then my ears, then it moved down my spine and out to the end of my tail.

By George! All at once I felt five years . . . lap, lap . . . twenty-five years younger! Boy, what a kick in the pants that stuff had! Woooooooo-eeee!

Lap, lap.

And by then, all the pieces of the puzzle had begun to fall into place. I had stumbled into an incredible scientific discovery, perhaps the most important discovery of the century.

ANYTHING THAT COULD STIMULATE A ROOT COULD REVIVE AND RESTORE A WORN-OUT RANCH DOG!

I was getting stronger by the minute. Was it just my imagination? No, surely not, for I could feel waves of thermonuclear energy moving through my body. I could hardly sit still. In fact, I began hopping around in a circle.

It happened that Drover came up at that very moment. He twisted his head to the side and gave me a puzzled look.

"Gosh, what's gotten into you? I thought you were worn to a frizzle."

"Ha, ha! That's the way it used to be, Drover, but no more. I've become a dymino of energy."

"I'll be derned. Must have been that grasshopper, huh?"

"Not at all, my friend, for you see . . ." Hmmm. All at once it occurred to me that . . . uh . . . there might be reasons, security reasons, for concealing the true nature of my test results.

I mean, we weren't 100% sure of our conclusions, right? And although Drover was a nice little mutt and a true friend, that didn't mean that I had to tell him everything.

Don't forget the old saying: A little knowledge is a dangerous thing.

And the other old saying: Russian fools jump in where angels fear the tread.

What did that mean? I wasn't sure exactly, but it was a wise old saying. Drover wasn't a Russian dog but he was definitely a fool.

The point is that Drover didn't need to know.

"Yes, you're exactly right, Drover. It was the grasshopper."

"I'll be derned. The one I ate must have been a dud."

"The one you ate wasn't big enough or green enough. It's the big green ones that contain the higher octane levels. By the way, Drover, would you care to wrestle?"

"Wrestle? I don't think so. It's too hot, and besides, this old leg . . ."

WHONK!

I jumped him, threw him over my shoulder, and pinned him to the ground. I just couldn't resist a chance to wrestle. I mean, I was burning up with vitality.

Drover whined for me to let him up, so I did and began looking around for another, shall we say, sparring partner. My eyes fell upon Pete, who had ventured outside Sally May's yard and was slinking across the gravel drive.

Heh, heh.

I threw all engines into Fast Forward, spun my paws on the gravel, and went roaring after Precious Kitty. He knew something was up. Perhaps he

G. L. Holmes

saw the fire in my eyes. He stopped in his tracks, humped his back, and began to hiss.

Heh, heh. Bad move.

Just before I got there, he figured out the obvious, that his hissing couldn't stop a freight train. He sold out and ran to the nearest tree.

On another occasion, he would have been safe in a tree—and as a matter of fact, on reaching the first limb, he turned a haughty little smirk at me and stuck out his tongue.

Ha, ha! Little did he know. I didn't stop at the base of the tree, fellers. I climbed that rascal, which caused panic and pandabearium amongst the kitties, so to speak. He screeched and hissed and climbed higher.

I followed. This was fun. I had never climbed a tree before. Whooo-pee! What a lark. Pete scratched and clawed his way out to the tiny branches at the end of a limb, and I . . . hmm, sort of ran out of structural support for my enormous body, you might say, and fell out of the tree.

Good thing old Slim was down there, greasing the trailer bearings, otherwise I might have hit the ground with a thud, but he was there and I landed on his head.

Boy, was he shocked. What a riot. Hat, glasses, bearings, and grease flew in all directions. That woke him up, I'll bet.

Whilst he stared at me with wide eyes, I gave him a huge lick on the face and went bounding away to find another source of entertainment.

"Good honk," I heard him say, "I just got hit by a falling dog!"

Right-toe! And I was just getting warmed up.

It was my good fortune just then to see seven pecking chickens up ahead of me. How perfect! You know how much I love to bulldoze chickens. It's one of the greatest thrills this life has to offer, even better than treeing cats, because the chickens flutter and flap and make a lot more noise than a cat.

ZOOM! SQUAWK, BAWK, BAWK, KA-BAWK!

Wow. It was great. Wonderful. Terrific. Feathers and chickens flew in all directions. It was one of the most meaningful experiences of my entire career.

The only trouble was that it ended in a matter of seconds, and once you've scattered all the chickens, fellers, it's hard to go back to life's dull routines.

I trotted past Slim and gave him a big grin. He was trying to wipe the axle grease off his glasses and he didn't look too happy about it.

"You dufus dog, what were you doing up in that tree?"

He would never understand. Nobody would understand. I had just discovered a secret energy source and had transformed myself into Turbo Pooch—half dog and half bulldozer.

As I approached Drover, he began backing away. "Hank, something's come over you. I think that grasshopper must have been eating dynamite and gasoline. I've never seen you act this way before. I'm kind of worried about you."

"Ha. Don't worry about me, kid. Worry about the rest of the world. Come on, let's wrestle some more. Let's go a few rounds of boxing. Let's run a five-mile race. Let's tear down a few trees."

He kept backing away. "You know, Hank, I'd love to do all that, but it's awful hot and this old leg's sure been giving me fits."

"Yeah? Well, let's just yank it off." His eyes crossed. I laughed. "Just kidding, Drover. Don't be so serious. Relax and enjoy life."

"How can I relax when you're acting so weird?"

"I don't know, pard. As a matter of fact, I'm having a little trouble relaxing myself. I mean, one hour ago I could hardly stay awake. Now, I can't find enough things to do to burn up all this energy."

"That was quite a grasshopper."

"A what? Oh yes, of course. The, uh, grasshopper. Yes indeed, that was quite a . . ." My ears shot up. They had just picked up the sounds of an Incoming Vehicle. "Come on, son, we've got an interception job to do. Hot dog!"

"Yeah, that's me. I'm a hot dog and I don't want to run, 'cause that'll just make me a hot dogger. I'll meet you around front."

I hit Full Throttle, spun all four paws on the gravel, and went ripping around the south side of the house. I intercepted the I.V. up by the shelter belt and provided escort all the way to the front of the machine shed.

Actually, I did more than that. I got bored with mere escort duty and began biting the front tires. Yes, I knew it was dangerous, but I didn't care. I seemed to have developed a taste for danger.

That's odd, isn't it? I mean, all this wild energy had come from a bucket of PLANT FOOD. By George, if that stuff had affected Sally May's shrubberies and flowers the way it affected me, they'd have been running all over the ranch.

Wouldn't that have been something to see, Sally May chasing her petunias and dragonsnappers and hollyhockers through the home pasture?

Well, I was having such a big time snapping at the tires that I didn't notice to who or whom the pickup belonged. Or to put it another way, I didn't notice that the driver was Billy, our neighbor to the east.

Do you remember Billy? Maybe not. The most important detail I can tell you about Billy is that he had several dogs, and one of them happened to be the most gorgeous collie gal in the whole world.

And you'll never guess who was sitting in the back of the pickup.

CHAPTER

6

I PREPARE TO THRASH THE NEIGHBORHOOD BULLY

By the time Billy stepped out of the pickup, I had already done Date and Mark on all four tires. I could tell that he was impressed.

He walked over to Slim, who was still sitting in the shade with a handful of grease and trailer bearings. "What have y'all been feeding that dog? In this heat, I can hardly get mine to scratch a flea. Old Hank's running around like a pup in January."

Slim shrugged. "Beats me. A little while ago, the crazy outfit chased the cat up this tree—and fell on top of me. I liked to have had a stroke. What's up?"

"Oh, I need to borrow some 6011 welding rod. You got any?"

"Well," he grunted and pushed himself up, "let's go see. Boy, it's hot. Makes a guy wish he could rent a big watermelon and move into it for the rest of the summer."

They shuffled into the machine shed. It was then that I turned my attention to the back of the pickup and saw . . . mercy! There she was, the girl of my dreams, just as I had seen her so many times in my slumbering sleepiness.

The dewberry eyes. The long collie nose. The flaxen hair. The perfect collie ears . . . holy smokes, my heart stopped beating and I forgot to breathe.

It was the lovely Miss Beulah.

After almost dying of joy and excitement, I snatched myself back from the brink of the edge and regained my composure. I wiggled my eyebrow three times and gave her my most swavv . . . swaav . . . swwaav . . . most charming smile.

"Well, my goodness! Hath the sun risen before us in the middle of the day or is this Miss Beulah the Collie?"

I shall never forget her words. She said, "Hello Hank."

Beautiful. Pure poetry. I could sense that she was still madly in love with me and that our romance would begin just where it had left off, just as though we had spent every minute . . .

Bird dog? There seemed to be a bird dog sitting on the opposite side of the pickup. He was giving me a lopsided grin.

"Hi Hank. By golly, it's great to see you again. How about this weather? You ever seen such heat? I haven't worked out all week."

That was Plato, of course, Plato the stick-tailed spotted bird dog. He spent his time pointing tennis shoes and retrieving sticks and thinking about birds. And what really ripped me was that Beulah seemed to like him.

I gave him a nod. "Yes, the heat has been terrible." I knocked off three back flips in a row, did a forward flip with a half-twist, and landed on my feet. "I've had to cut back on my work schedule too."

You should have seen his eyes! They almost bugged out of his head. "Good gravy, Hank, that's very impressive, very impressive. Beulah, did you see that?"

She did. I knew she did because I could see and almost feel her adoring gaze on me. So, just for the heck of it, I knocked off three forwardses, two backwardses, landed on my front legs, did five pushups, and ended with five carbuncles. Cartwheels.

Plato almost fell out of the pickup. He couldn't believe his eyes. "Wow. By golly. Hank, I'm really impressed. No kidding. I mean, in this heat the rest of us just drag around and try to survive, but you . . . did you see that, Honey Bun?"

"Quit calling her Honey Bun."

I froze and cocked my ear. Was I hearing voices? Unless I was badly mistaken, I had just heard someone say, "Quit calling her Honey Bun."

I shot a glance at Plato. His expression had changed. His eyes showed . . . fear. I shifted my gaze towards Beulah. She was looking away, as though . . . hmmm. Very strange.

Plato cut his eyes from side to side and motioned for me to come over. When I did, he glanced over his shoulder and dropped his voice to a whisper.

"Hank, there's something I must tell you. Remember Rufus, Billy's Doberman pinscher? He's sitting up there on the spare tire."

"Oh. So that was his voice I heard?"

"Right. Yes. Exactly. He forced me and Beulah to sit in opposite corners. He doesn't want us to be friendly, if you know what I mean, because he thinks Beulah likes him."

"Hmmm. Does she?" I turned to Beulah.

"I can't stand him," she whispered. "He's an ugly toad, and he's a bully and a brute, and he's so mean to poor Plato . . . oh, I hate him!"

"I'll be derned. Well, maybe I need to have a talk with old Rufie."

Plato's eyes grew wide, and he shook his head. "No, don't get involved, Hank. I know you mean well, but this is just something we have to live with. We can stand it another day, can't we, Honey . . . er, can't we, Beulah?"

"Stay on your side, bird brain, and quit talking to my sweetie pie." It was The Voice again.

"Okay, Rufus, sorry. It won't happen again." Plato turned back to me. "You see what I mean? He's the meanest, most overbearing dog I've ever known. And I'll be honest, Hank. He scares me."

"I wonder what he'd do if I yelled . . . honey bun."

Plato flinched at the words. "Oh, I wouldn't do that, Hank, really. No kidding. To you it might be a joke, but Rufus has no sense of humor at all. And let me remind you, Hank, this guy has hurt a lot of dogs. He's vicious."

"I'll swan." I threw back my head and called, "Honey bun, here honey bun. Oh honey bun. Here a honey, there a bun, everywhere a honey bun."

Plato gasped. "No, Hank, please . . ."

"Honey bun, honey bun, honey bun!"

Plato's eyes rolled back in his head. Beulah's eyelids sank. The pickup lurched and bounced, and Rufus's ugly head appeared above the tailgate.

I gave him a lazy grin. "Hi. How y'all today?"

He spoke in a deep booming voice. "Who said 'honey bun'?"

"Well, let's see. It wasn't Plato. It wasn't Beulah, so perhaps 'twas I."

"Who are you?"

"Fine, thanks. How about yourself?"

He roasted me with his eyes. "I said, WHO are you, smart guy. I don't care how you are."

"Oh, sorry. Hank the Cowdog. You're on my ranch."

"Oh yeah. I whipped you once—on your ranch. It was fun but it didn't last long." He aimed a paw at me. "Don't say those words again. I don't like 'em."

"You mean 'honey bun'?"

"That's right. I hate 'em."

"Honey bun."

There was a long moment of silence. Then, "Are you trying to be funny or are you just stupid?"

"No, every time I see Beulah's lovely face, I think of honey buns. Odd, isn't it?"

"I ought to knock your block off. Don't ever say 'honey bun' to my honey bun."

"Oh, she's yours, huh?"

"Right." He turned to Beulah. "Aren't you, Honey Bun?" She turned away and didn't answer. He laughed. "She's crazy about me, and even if she ain't, that's too bad. She's mine, so butt out before you get hurt. You got that?"

"Nope."

His eyes widened. "What?"

"Rufus, there's something we need to discuss. I don't like you."

A grin spread over his mouth. "Yeah? That's nice."

"And it's not just because you have the ugliest face I've ever seen." His smile began to wilt. "You can't help it that you're ugly and stupid. What I don't like is that you're rude."

"Oh yeah?"

"Uh huh. And you're being rude to a lady friend of mine—on my ranch. That's not very nice."

"Big deal."

"If you'll apologize to Beulah and promise to be a good little doggie for the rest of your life, I'll forget the whole thing."

"You must be crazy."

"If you aren't dog enough to apologize to the lady, I'll be forced to thrash you right here in front of everyone. It's up to you."

Beulah stared at me with terror-stricken eyes. Plato was shaking his head and wheezing and trying to motion me to be quiet.

Rufus leaned over the tailgate and narrowed his ugly bloodshot eyes. "Say, bub, I beat up cowdogs just for exercise, and then I move on to the tough guys. Be kind to yourself and get lost."

"Honey bun."

There was a long throbbing moment of silence as we glared into each other's eyes. Plato couldn't stand it any longer.

"Settle down, Rufus, easy now. Hank has a great sense of humor but sometimes . . ."

"Shut up. Get back in your corner."

"Right, okay, but let me emphasize . . ."

"Shut up!"

Plato did as he was told. Rufus's terrible eyes swung back to me. "Where would you like your whipping, up here in the pickup or down there on the ground?"

"Tell you what, Rufe, let me get a drink of water and I'll think about it. Don't go away."

As I turned to leave, I heard him laugh. "Wave goodbye to your hero. He won't be back."

I trotted down to the yard gate. Heh, heh. Little did old Rufus know that I had a secret weapon. Heh, heh. A couple of slurps of root stimulator and . . .

The bucket was gone!

CHAPTER

7

POISONED BY MOPWATER

Cold fear began working its way down my back and out to the end of my tail. Behind me, I heard Rufus laughing and calling out insults.

"Hurry up, Hero. I'm gettin' bored."

Gulp. Now what? Who had moved my bucket? Where did it go? My eyes searched the entire backyard area. I could feel my reserves of energy slipping away, and all at once I became aware of the heat. It was so hot!

I had to find the bucket. My reputation, my whole career was at stake because . . . holy smokes, I had just spent the last fifteen minutes mouthing off to one of the meanest dogs in Texas!

I was on the brink of despair and desolation when the back door opened and Sally May stepped out on the porch. In her right hand she carried . . . the bucket. Yes, the very same bucket. I identified it at once.

She set it down on the porch. Boy, what a relief! There for a minute, I had feared the worst, that she had poured out my supply of precious root stimulator and wasted it on a bunch of idiot plants.

But there it was, safe and sound, and now all I had to do . . . mop? Why was she dipping a mop into my . . .

And then the terrible truth came crashing down upon my head. She had poured out my Precious Root Stimulator and was using the container as a MOP BUCKET!

Oh, what a cruel fate, to be brought down in the prime of my life by a mop!

"Hurry up, cowdog. We're waiting."

Sally May squeezed out the mop with both hands and went back into the house. She left the bucket on the porch. I found myself . . . staring at it.

It was the same bucket I had drunk out of before, right? It contained mopwater instead of root stimulator, but both were liquids, composed primarily of water, which means they were very similar.

If root stimulator and mopwater were very similar, then perhaps they were almost the same. Who would know the difference? Not a plant. Not a mop.

I mean, the little cotton strands on a mop were almost identical to the roots on a plant. Both were long and stringy, both extended downward, both were attached to a longer stalk or stick, which extended upward.

Hencely, by following the twisted path of logic, I had arrived at the startling conclusion that mopwater and root stimulator were exactly the same stuff, which meant that mopwater would restore my reserves of energy just as the plant food had.

Gee whiz, what a breakthrough, what a triumph of scientific thinking over the rubble of ordinary experience.

Only one small problem remained, and it was only a small problem. I would have to make a penetration of Sally May's yard. That was no big deal. I'd done it before, many times, and though it posed certain risks, I knew I could do it—because I HAD to do it.

"Hey cowdog, snap it up, will ya?"

I coiled my legs under me and went flying over the yard fence. I landed on silent paws, stopped in my tracks, and listened. I could hear Sally May's voice inside the house. She seemed to be discussing something with Little Alfred . . . yes, they were discussing spilled milk.

She would never know that I had broken into her yard and borrowed some, uh, Mop Stimulator.

I crept forward. Two steps. Stop. Listen. Three steps. Stop. Listen. Four steps. And suddenly I was there, standing on the porch with the bucket looming before me.

I shot glances over both shoulders, plunged my head into the bucket, and began lapping the . . . stuff tasted pretty awful, but it's common knowledge that good medicine always tastes bad, and . . .

BONK!

Who would have thought that she would finish her mopping and spilled milk lecture so soon? Not me. I was totally shocked when the screen door flew open and struck me on the left shoulder, and it appeared that I had been caught with my head in the, uh, cookie jar.

Mop bucket.

Our eyes met. I licked a drip off my chin and tried to squeeze up a smile that would . . . uh, well . . . explain exactly what I was doing there . . . in her yard . . . on her back porch . . . in her mop bucket.

Hi Sally May. I know this looks odd—even strange—but I think I can explain everything.

She stared at me for a long throbbing moment. Then she leaned down and spoke. "You. Are Drinking. Mopwater."

Yes, I, uh, knew that.

"And before that, you were drinking my plant food."

Right, and there was a reason for that too. No kidding.

"What is wrong with you? Can't you find a drink of plain water on this ranch?"

Sure, but . . .

"There's a creek right over there and it's full of fresh drinking water."

Yes, I . . . I was aware of the . . . uh . . . creek.

She brought her face right down to the level of my nose. "Will you please stop behaving like a moron?"

I knew in my deepest heart that she wouldn't approve of a mopwater kiss at that particular moment, but some strange urge caused my tongue to shoot out and give her a big juicy lick on the . . . well, on the nose-mouth region of her face.

Good grief, you'd have thought she'd been bitten by a cobra, the way she drew back. And screeched. Yes, she screeched at me, and then came the mop. Splat! Right across my face.

G.L.Holmes

Well, I could take a hint. If she didn't want me around . . . SPLAT! . . . I would just . . . SPLAT! . . . run for my life and let the chipmunks fall where they would.

I made it over the yard fence just one step ahead of the Murderous Mop and took refuge in some tall weeds. There, I heard her say, "I'll swear, that is the dumbest dog!"

Boy, that hurt—not as much as the mop, but it opened wounds deep inside my heart and soul.

Wounds that might never heal.

She went back inside the house. She probably didn't realize that her cutting remarks had inflicted irreruptable damage to our relationship.

And she probably didn't even care.

"Hey cowdog, we're waitin'."

The sound of Rufus's voice brought me back to the other crisis in my life. Had the mopwater done its job? I had to know the truth.

I turned to Data Control for a report on all internal systems. My heart sank as I scanned the report flashing across the screen of my mind. It showed low readings in all departments: heart rate, blood sugar, oxygen-acetylene supply, energy, ambition, and cellular phonography.

Even more disturbing was the presence of high levels of toxic mopwater in the stomach area. Burp. My poor stomach had certainly been tested: a gooey green grasshopper, root stimulator, and now mopwater.

Did I feel sick? Sure, but I didn't have time to be sick. My career and reputation were hanging in the ballast. I had talked my way into a fight I couldn't possibly win, yet I couldn't walk away from it either.

Well . . . obviously it was time for a song, right? I mean, there comes a time in every dog's life when he bursts into singing because, well, the other things he might be doing aren't so great.

Have we ever done "The Mopwater Song"? Maybe not. Here's how it goes.

The Mopwater Song

I never should have drunk that
 mopwater,
Never should, never should,
 mopwater.
Never should have tried that
 mopwater.
Mopwater, slopwater, sick as a
 horse.

Mopwater is low in calories,
But it's also low in taste.
It will fill your daily requirement
Of spiderwebs, dirt, and various
 wastes.

Never should have sampled yucky
 dirty mopwater,
Silly dog, stupid dog, mopwater.
A belly ache can come from
 drinking mopwater.
Belly trouble, tummy rumble,
 stomach upset.

If you're preparing to fight a
    gorilla,

Exercise caution and stay on
    your toes.

If somebody says mopwater will
    help you,

He's telling a lie, so punch him
    in the nose.

I never should have drunk that
    mopwater,

Never should, never should,
    mopwater.

Never should have tried that
    mopwater.

Mopwater, slopwater, sick as a
    horse.

Not bad, huh? I mean, for a song that I just threw together at the last moment, it was pretty derned good.

Well, I gathered my few remaining shreds of energy—boy, it was hot—and made the long trudge up the hill. There was Billy's pickup, just where I had left it.

Rufus spotted me right away. His pointed ears shot up and a wicked sneer worked its way across his toothy mouth.

"Well! Look who's coming back. How was the water, pal? I hope it was good, 'cause it may be the last drink you'll ever get."

I felt the harsh glare of the afternoon sun as I dragged myself to the rear of the pickup. I caught a glimpse of Plato and Beulah. Their eyes showed the terror of what was about to happen. They knew, just as I knew, that I was about to march into a Battle of No Return.

It had to be done. I had talked my way into this deal and I couldn't back down. It was rotten luck that my supply of root stimulator had lasted just long enough to get me into a world of trouble, but that was life.

When you're Head of Ranch Security, you don't make excuses.

I jumped up into the pickup. The effort of getting there left me drained. The sun was burning me up, wilting me, sucking the energy out of my muscles and bones.

I lifted my head and looked Shark Face in the eyes. "Okay, Rufus, I guess it's time."

His laugh sent shivers down my spine.

C H A P T E R

8

HIGHER DUTY CALLS ME TO BATTLE

You probably think that I went into deadly combat against Rufus and got myself thrashed. Or maybe you think that I thrashed him—a long shot, I'll admit, but strange things happen in this old world.

Well, the truth is that neither happened. Rufus and I were in the Preliminary Growls Stage of the big fight when, much to my surprise and relief, Slim and Billy came walking out of the machine shed and saw us.

"Say, Slim, you'd better get old Hank out of my pickup before Rufus eats him up."

Slim came at a run—okay, not exactly a run but maybe a trot. He reached over the tailgate, grabbed me by the tail, and began pulling me backwards.

I must admit that his sudden appearance made me feel somewhat bolder. When he began pulling me backward, I locked down all four legs, leaned toward Rufus, and added a little volume to my growling. It had kind of a nice effect, the growling plus the screech of my claws on the floor of the pickup bed.

"Well, it looks like they've saved you this time, Rufus. One more minute and they never would have pulled me off."

"Ha! One more minute and they wouldn't have found you, jerk, 'cause you'd have been sawdust."

"You're a big talker, Rufus, and we know you're the champ at beating up widows and orphans, but one of these days . . ."

His eyes lit up. "Yeah? One of these days . . . what? Come on, cowdog, don't stutter. Name the day and time."

"Well, I . . ."

"Meet me this afternoon on the hill above my place."

"Today? I'd have to, uh, check my . . ."

"Four o'clock. That gives you two hours to get there."

"Well, I . . . that's the hottest part of the day, and don't you think . . ."

"Be there. And if you ain't there, you're nothing but a yella chicken and I'll be twice as mean to your girlfriend and it'll be your fault."

By that time Slim had gotten a good grip on me and lifted me out of the pickup. Billy said goodbye and drove away. Rufus was sitting on his spare tire, looking like a king on his throne, while Beulah waved a sad goodbye and Plato squeezed himself deeper into his corner.

When the sounds of the motor faded in the distance, Slim looked down at me and shook his head.

"Well, you dodged a cannonball there, pooch. If I hadn't come out just when I did, we'd be searching for your bodily parts right now."

Yes, I . . . uh . . . realized that, although . . .

"It ain't smart to pick fights with the heavyweight champion of the neighborhood, and some people would even say it's dumb." He reached down and scratched me behind the ears. "But just between us dogs, I'm kind of proud of you for thinkin' about it. I never did care for that hateful thing. How about a little reward?"

I perked up at that. Yes, a little reward would be nice. Or even a big reward.

"I'd sure like to buy you a steak."

A steak? That might work.

"Only I ain't got one, so how about doubles on dog food?"

Plain old ordinary dry dog food? Gee, I had hoped . . .

"Special Deluxe Co-op Hot Rod Ration. How does that sound?"

Well, not as good as a steak but . . . Hot Rod Ration, huh? It might be all right.

We went to the machine shed.

As you may know, we dogs ate our dog food from an overturned Ford hubcap. Slim poured it full of this exotic new type of dog food and I began crunching.

I soon realized that he had been exercising his sense of humor. It was the same old stuff—hard, dry kernels that tasted like a mixture of sawdust and stale grease.

I beamed him a wounded look which said, "This is it? No steak?"

"That's the best we've got, pooch. Take it or leave it. Just because you had one heroic thought don't mean you get to dine at Mrs. Astor's table."

Fine. I would collect my measly little reward and go on about my life. Double dog food wasn't a steak, but it beat a poke in the eye with a sharp stick. And who was Mrs. Astor anyway?

I was crunching my way through the heap of dry, tasteless kernels when Drover poked his head out of the machine shed. He glanced to the left and to the right, then came creeping out.

"Hi Hank. What you doing?"

"I'm trying to eat . . ." Crunch, crunch. ". . . petrified camel droppings."

"I'll be derned. It looks just like dog food to me."

"Some people call it that."

"Can I have a bite?"

"No." Crunch, crunch. "By the way, Drover, where were you when the fighting broke out?"

"Well, let's see. I guess I took a wrong turn and sort of ended up in the machine shed."

"I see. Did it occur to you that I might need your help?"

"Oh yeah, but by the time I made it to the machine shed, this old leg was about to kill me. See?" He limped around in a circle. "Terrible pain. But I heard the whole thing."

"What did you think?"

"I thought . . ." He looked up at the sky. "I thought you'd lost your mind and were fixing to lose your life, is what I thought."

"As a matter of fact, Drover, that's closer to the truth than you might suppose." I told him the whole story about the root stimulator.

"I'll be derned. I thought you got all that energy from the grasshopper."

"No, the stupid grasshopper almost strangled me, thanks to you and your bonehead ideas."

"Mine was pretty good. Tasted like chicken."

"Mine did NOT taste like chicken, and it did NOT give me one bit of energy."

"Oh well. Everything turned out all right. You didn't have to fight Rufus and now it's all behind you."

I lifted my head from the bowl and stared at the runt. "What do you mean, it's all behind me?"

"Well, let's see here. The world's divided up into what's up front and what's behind. What's behind is over and what's up front is under, and . . . I think I'm getting confused."

"Didn't you hear what he said? He challenged me to a duel in two hours. In other words, it's not over yet."

"Oh, that. Yeah, I heard it but I knew you wouldn't be dumb enough to show up. Tee hee hee. Boy, that would be about the dumbest thing in the world, going down to . . . " His eyes popped open. "Hank, you wouldn't do such a thing . . . would you?"

I paced several steps away and looked off into the distance. "Drover, what I'm about to say might shock you."

"Then maybe we could talk about something else."

"There are times when my position as Head of Ranch Security becomes a heavy burden. It's not just a job, you see. It's a calling, a mission."

"I went fishin' once."

"I'm judged by standards unknown to ordinary dogs, standards that are sometimes almost impossible to attain."

"Yeah, and that's time to quit."

"Exactly. It's a heavy load indeed. Drover, have you ever heard of the ancient Samurai?"

"Oh yeah. It's a steak house in Amarillo."

"What?"

"I said . . . well, let's see here. I said, 'they house snakes in Amarillo.'"

"No, no. It has nothing to do with snakes."

"Oh good. I'm scared of snakes."

"And they don't operate out of Amarillo. The Samurai were a society of warriors who lived in some strange faraway land."

"California?"

"Right. Something like that. And they lived by a higher code than ordinary people, Drover. They were warriors who protected the innocent, fought for justice, and devoted their lives to righting wrong."

"I always wanted to be a writer."

"And so it is with the Head of Ranch Security. We are droven, Drivel, by a higher duty."

"My name's Drover."

"We must do, not merely what is safe and comfortable, but what is right."

"I think I've got a novel in me somewhere."

"What?"

"I said . . . well, let's see here. Oh yeah. I think I've got a novel in me somewhere."

"Open your mouth." He did and I looked inside. "No, that's called the Ulterior Punching Bagus, so named because it resembles a little punching bag."

"I'll be derned. Maybe I ought to try boxing."

"Exactly." I tried to pick up my train of thought. "What were we talking about?"

"Mopwater, I think."

"Oh yes. It was once believed that mopwater could restore energy and so forth, but that's not what we were talking about, Drover, and I'm beginning to wonder if you've been listening."

"Oh yeah, I heard it all. Something about a guy named Sam who traded snakes in Amarillo."

"No, not Sam. Rufus. And let's skip to the bottom line because frankly, Drover, I'm beginning to find this conversation a little confusing."

"Yeah, me too."

"The bottom line is that honor and duty demand that I accept Rufus's challenge and fight a duel to the death."

"That's the dumbest thing I ever heard."

"What?"

"I said, oh boy. Good. Yippee.

"Thanks, Drover, but there's more."

Do I dare reveal the rest? Hang on and let me think about it.

CHAPTER

9

MADAME MOONSHINE IS CAPTURED BY CANNIBALS

Think. Think. Think.

Heavy duty contemplation in progress.

Please hold.

Caution: dogs at work.

All circuits are busy at the moment.

Hot tamales for ninety-eight cents.

Thought session completed.

Okay, there we go. I guess it wouldn't hurt to let you in on the startling revelation I revealed to Drover.

I began pacing back and forth in front of him, as I often do when my mind is racing. "You see, Drover, I am driven by this devotion to truth and honor."

"Yeah, and that beats walking."

"Exactly. And truth and honor demand that I accept Rufus's challenge. To do otherwise would be . . . what's the word I'm searching for?"

"Smart?"

"No."

"Beet farmer?"

"No."

"Pineapple?"

I gave him a withering glare. "Drover, if you can't contribute anything to this conversation, just be quiet."

"Well, you asked."

"I'm sorry I asked."

"That's okay. I couldn't help it."

"Shut up." I probed the vapors and smoke upon the volcano of my . . . something. "Okay, here we go. I must accept the challenge and go into combat against Rufus. The problem is that I'm totally unprepared for such an ordeal and would probably be slaughtered."

"That's a problem, all right."

"Hence, to prepare myself for this fateful mission, I must leave the ranch, go out into the wilderness, and search for strength and courage, just as the Samurai did in Ancient California."

"Rotsaruck."

"And Drover, I'd like for you to go along as my second."

"Your second what?"

"My second. That's what it's called. You'd be my second."

"That's not much time."

"It has nothing to do with time. It's a position. You'd be my second in command."

"Oh good. I think I can handle that."

"Great. I like your attitude. In the event that I'm slaughtered in the early going, you'll take my place."

His eyes crossed and suddenly he began limping around in a circle. "Oh my gosh, this leg just went out! Oh, the pain! Rush me to the machine shed, stand back, I'm fixing to . . ."

My goodness. He fainted. I mean, he just collapsed on the ground, with all four legs sticking straight up in the air. I rushed to his side.

"Speak to me, Drover. What's happened?"

"Leg attack. Worst one ever. Terrible pain. Don't think I can make the trip to the wilderness. Go on without me."

"And leave you here in this state?"

"Yeah, I'd rather suffer in Texas. I'll be all right . . . if I can stand the guilt. That's the worst part of staying home, trying to live with the guilt."

"Well, be brave. And Drover, if I should happen not to return . . . " I ran my gaze over the place I had loved and protected for so many years. " . . . take good care of the ranch. Good-bye, old friend, and good luck."

And with that, I tore myself away from home and friends, turned and ran away from the voice inside my head that urged me to take the path of leased resistance. Sure, it would have been easier to stay home and forget about Beulah and Plato, honor and duty, and the higher calling of my profession.

But that's not what cowdogs do.

I ran until I could run no more. Finding myself alone in brush along the creek, I stopped and caught my breath. I was panting. The heat was terrible. Who could think of fighting a duel in such heat?

And what the heck? Maybe I could . . .

No. I had to fulfill my mission, even if that meant . . . I walked to the creek's edge and drank my fill of cool sweet water. It was a refreshing change from mopwater.

Having drinked my fill . . . having drank . . . having drunk . . . having lapped up all the water I could hold, I set a course to the east, threading my way through the dense underwear of tamaracks and willows.

Undergrowth, actually. Dense undergrowth.

All the familiar sounds, sights, and smells of civilization faded into the distance, and were replaced by others that were new and strange: dark shadows, the cries of birds overhead, the swish and slither of I-knew-not-what in the brush around me.

I had reached the wilderness, an area into which I had seldom ventured during my career—and for good reason. Here, I was unknown and unwanted; a stranger, an intruder into an ancient rhythm of which I was not a part. Of which.

I hurried along. Suddenly a twig snapped. I whirled to my left and faced . . . not much, just a clump of brush. Perhaps I had stepped on the twig myself, but my nerves were on edge, don't you see, and . . . it was kind of spooky, and I'll admit that I was feeling a bit uneasy.

Nervous.

Alert to danger.

Okay, scared, but if you'd been there, you would have been scared too. A guy never knew what manner of creature or monster he might encounter in this part of the ranch.

I continued my journey. I knew where I was going: to Madame Moonshine's cave in those bluffs just west of the Parnell water gap. If you recall, Madame Moonshine was a wise little owl who claimed to have magical powers. I'd never been entirely convinced that she had "magical" powers, but she had gotten me out of a few scrapes in the past, and I hoped she might help me out of this one.

I slowed my pace and began studying the landmarks. There was the big cottonwood tree that had been struck by lightning. That was familiar. And yes, there were the bluffs on the south side of the creek. I was getting close.

I began to feel some better, now that I had . . . huh? I stopped in my tracks. Unless my ears were playing tricks on me, I had just heard . . . something. I lifted my ears to Maximum Gathering Mode and homed in on the sound.

Voices? Laughter? Impossible. Nobody laughed out here in this wilderness . . . unless . . . gulp. I began to realize to who or whom those voices might belong—a couple of renegade outlaws who were right at home in the wilderness, and the wildernesser it was, the better they liked it.

I crouched down, peered through the tamarack brush, and listened. And yes, there they were—Rip and Snort, the dreaded cannibal brothers. That in itself was bad enough, me stumbling into their camp in the middle of a trackless wilderness.

But there was more. I had come to seek advice from Madame Moonshine, right? Well, guess who was sitting in the middle of the cannibals—tied up with a piece of grapevine.

Madame Moonshine herself, and it appeared that she might need my help even more than I needed hers, because the cannibals were wearing huge grins and licking their chops, as though they were working themselves up for a big feathery feast.

The thought crossed my mind that I should creep away from here and go flying back to headquarters. They hadn't seen me yet and seemed pretty absorbed in heckling Madame Moonshine. And didn't I have enough problems of my own without taking on any of Madame's? And besides, she was supposed to have magical powers, right? So why didn't she use them to save herself?

In the interest of truth and so forth, I'll admit that I did take two steps backward . . . three steps . . . okay, five or six steps backwards, but then I caught myself and felt ashamed. Was I really enough of a cad to run away and leave that poor little owl to her fate?

Well, I was enough of a cad to *think* about it, but not enough of one to actually do it. I returned to my listening post and . . . well, listened, of course.

What else would you do in a listening post?

I guess you could watch and listen both, and in fact, that's exactly what I did. I crouched down in the sand, peered through the low branches of a tamarack bush, and observed the proceedings.

As you will see, that turned out to be a fitful decision.

Faithful.

Fateful.

Phooey.

You'll find out soon enough, and it just might scare you out of your wits.

No kidding.

See, I know what's fixing to happen and you don't. If I were in your shoes, I'd . . . well, look pretty funny, wouldn't I, because dogs don't wear shoes.

A little humor there.

But I'd also think twice about going on with the story, is the point, because we're coming to the scary part.

Maybe you'd better quit and go on to bed.

C H A P T E R

10

THE SINGING
IGNORAMUSES

I knew you wouldn't take my advice. You think you're pretty tough, don't you? Well, maybe you are and maybe you're not. We'll see about that.

But don't say you weren't warned.

Okay, where were we? The cannibal brothers had Madame Moonshine tied up and they were staring and grinning at her. And licking their chops in what you might call a threatening manner.

See, I knew all their manniserums, because I had been in that same hot seat before, many times. Mannerisms, I should say, not manniserums. When a cannibal looks at you in a certain way, with a glint in his eye and with drooling chops, you begin to suspect that he's hungry.

And when two of 'em look at you that way, you know you've found Double Trouble.

Anyways, I tuned into their frequencies and listened. Madame was showing spunk and courage. She held her head up and glared right back at them.

"This is disgraceful! I demand that you turn me loose, right now and this very minute." The brothers grinned. "Because if you don't release me and put an end to this disgraceful folly, I shall have to employ drastic measures."

"Har, har, har."

"And if I am forced to do so, you will regret it."

"Har, har, har."

"Very well. You leave me no choice. I will now summon my bodyguard. Timothy! Oh Timothy! Come, Timothy, come at once and give these ruffians a taste of their own medicine."

At that very moment, I heard a slithering sound behind me, and then felt something . . . uh . . . cold and creepy moving along my right side. I didn't really want to know what it might be, but my eyes sort of wandered to the right and . . .

Yipes! I found myself looking straight into the eyes of the biggest, ugliest rattlesnake I'd seen since the last time I'd crossed paths with Big Tim, Madame Moonshine's personal bodyguard.

He gave me a glare that sent pins and needles down my backbone. Oh, and he stuck out his tongue. On impulse, I pushed his head away.

"Will you point that thing somewhere else, you dumbbell snake! The guys you want are right over there in the clearing." His tail began to rattle. "What I meant to say was . . . hi, Tim, how's it going, fella, and the ruffians are straight ahead and to the left."

He continued to rattle and glare at me.

"I'm really not part of this deal, Tim, no kidding. I'm just an innocent bystander who's . . . uh . . . innocently standing by, so to speak. And you're looking for coyotes, right? Over there. See, I may look like a coyote but I'm actually a dog. Honest. No kidding."

He was still rattling.

"Okay, forget what I said about you being a dumbbell snake. You're not a dumbbell snake at all. You're one of the nicest, sweetest . . ."

Madame's voice cut me off. "Timothy! Come here at once."

Big Tim gave me one last hateful look and slithered into battle, whilst I finished my thought—under my breath, of course. "You're one of the ugliest dumbbell snakes I ever met."

Well, Big Tim made his appearance on the scenery. Madame Moonshine smiled at the brothers and announced, "And this is Timothy, my personal bodyguard. As you can see, he is a turbocharged western diamondback rattlesnake, and he is armed with the very deadliest of poisons."

Rip and Snort winked at each other and grinned. "Coyote brothers not even tinier bit scared of bodyguarded snake."

"Well, you should be. Why, Timothy once spat upon an enormous tree and it withered and died, before our very eyes. What he might do to a couple of unkempt, ill-mannered ragamuffin coyotes, we can only imagine."

They laughed again. "Ha! Ragamuffin coyotes not worrying about fat stupid snake. Ragamuffin coyotes wrap fatter stupidest snake around tree and tie in knot, ho ho."

Madame gave them a wise smile. "Oh you think you will, do you? I think not. Timothy?" He threw himself into a coil, began buzzing, and pointed his head at the brothers. "Timothy, we are being harassed by these ignoramuses. Show them what we think of ignoramuses. Charge! Tallyho!"

By George, it was one of the shortest fights in history. In a matter of seconds, Rip and Snort had old Timothy wrapped around a hackberry tree and tied in a knot. He looked like a Christmas wreath.

I told you those guys were tough.

They returned to Madame Moonshine, who wasn't looking quite as spunky as she had before. Snort grinned down at her.

"What Momma Moonbeam think of ignoramuses now?"

She blinked her big owlish eyes. "I think you are ill-mannered, foul-smelling, uncivilized ruffians." They howled with glee. They loved it. "I think you should be ashamed of yourselves." More laughter.

C. L. Holmes

"But I can see that you're not, because you're nothing but a couple of ignorant barbarians."

They nodded their heads and laughed. "Coyote not give hoot for being ashamed. Coyote not give hoot for nothing. Ignoramus coyote brothers prouder and proudest, 'cause Rip and Snort love being ignor-rent."

And with that, the brothers cut loose with a song. I know, it was an odd time for them to burst into a song, but those guys were pretty strange. Here's how it went:

We're Proud To Be Ignoramuses

A cannibal's life's the one for us,
We're as happy as we can be.
We've got no job or worries
Or responsibilities.
We ain't too swift on thinking,
We ain't too sharp in math.
We're experts, though, at stinking
'Cause we never take a bath.

We're proud to be ignoramuses,
Ramuses, ramuses.
We just love being ignoramuses,
It's more fun than a barrel of monkeys.

Me and Rip never went to school
Or learned arithmetic.
But we've got our own method for
    counting
And it works out pretty slick.
We point with our toes and call
    out the count,
"One, four, seven."
And if someone says, "You guys
    can't count,"
We beat him up. It works. Ho, ho.

We're proud to be ignoramuses,
Ramuses, ramuses.
We just love being ignoramuses,
It's more fun than a barrel of
    monkeys.

We're ignor-rent of language
And proud of it to boot.
We're fluent in burping and
    belching
And we don't give a hoot.
And as for the writing of portry
    and songs
With rhyming and rhythm and
    stuff.

We do if we want and don't if we
    don't,
And if you don't like it we'll break
    your face.

We're proud to be ignoramuses,
Ramuses, ramuses.
We just love being ignoramuses,
It's more fun than a barrel of
    monkeys.

We're proud to be ignoramuses,
It expresses our deepest thoughts.
We figger we're both getting
    famouses
For the science of mental rot.
And one of these days we'll win an
    award.
You weenies'll be so surprised.
Not the Nobel or Pulitzer,
But the Ignoramus Prize, ha ha.

We're proud to be ignoramuses,
Ramuses, ramuses.
We just love being ignoramuses,
It's more fun than a barrel of
    monkeys.

When they had finished singing the . . . uh . . . song . . . whatever it was . . . when they had finished their latest piece of coyote trash, they yipped and whooped, howled and hollered and hopped, leaped and jumped and congratulated each other for being such wonderful singers and composers.

Then they turned toothy grins on Madame. "What little owl think now of Ripping and Snort?"

She rolled her eyes and gave her head a shake. "That was the worst song I ever heard, or ever dreamed of hearing."

Their grins wilted. "Song not worst. Song gooder and goodest. Song expresserating deepest thoughts of ignoramus coyote brothers."

"It was so bad, you may very well have set all music back fifty years."

"Little owl better not talking trash about coyote music, 'cause Rip and Snort berry greater singest in whole world. Also hungry for owl supper, oh boy."

"If you're such good singers and if your song was so wonderful, why did those weeds over there begin to wilt in the middle of your song?"

All eyes swung to the north, to a small patch of careless weeds. By George, they had all withered and died.

"Ha! Must be pretty strong music, killing weeds."

"Yes indeed. Poisonous is the word."

"Ruffian brothers not give a hoot for weeds, ready insteader for supper of fresh owl."

Their yellow eyes began to sparkle and their tongues swept across their respective mouths. I was watching all of this from my hiding place in the brush, and I kept waiting for Madame to . . . well, DO SOMETHING. Why was she just sitting there? I mean, she had magical powers. Why wasn't she using them?

Those were all interesting questions, but it suddenly occurred to me that Rip and Snort were fixing to make a meal out of her, and never mind the interesting questions. Unless someone took charge of the situation and . . .

Gee, I sure hated to lose a friend like Madame Moonshine, but I wasn't the kind of dog who made a habit of butting into the affairs of . . . well, hungry cannibals.

I mean, it wasn't my fight. I had problems of my own, and as a matter of fact, I had BIG problems of my own and . . .

But on the other hand, the brothers were creeping towards her with a kind of evil lightning crackling in their eyes. I could see that Madame was afraid, but I kind of admired the way she held her head up and faced her destiny.

She had spunk and courage, that little owl, and it was just a shame . . .

I pushed myself up on all fours and walked into the middle of the gathering.

C H A P T E R

11

I MANAGE TO SAVE
MADAME MOONSHINE

See, I'd come up with an idea. Whether or not it was a good idea remained to be seen. It was the kind of idea a guy comes up with on the spurt of the moment and on short notice.

It was based on something Rip and Snort had revealed about themselves in their song: They were ignoramuses.

With a cover of boldness that covered the terror in my deepest innards, I went striding into the clearing, took a stand in front of the brothers, and stopped them with a raised paw.

"Halt!" They halted and stared at me with big puzzled eyeballs. "Rip, Snort, we don't have much time, so listen carefully. That song you just sang released a cloud of deadly poisonous gas over this whole area. We've got to get you out of here before . . . "

I pointed towards the wilted weeds. "Uh oh, it's already begun to work. You see? The fauna and floride have begun to die. The weeds will be the first to go, followed minutes later by trees and bushes, followed minutes later by animals, birds, and fish."

The brothers exchanged long glances.

"Guys, I've got to put the entire ranch under Emergency Poison Alert and I'm glad I found you before it was too late. I'm clearing out this whole section of the ranch, immediately, at once."

Snort scowled at me. "Coyote brothers not wanting cleared out to be."

"I know, Snort, but this poison is like nothing we've ever encountered before."

The brothers went into a whisper conference. I counted my heartbeats, hoping . . .

"Rip and Snort just fixing to eat little owl, not wanting to leave good nourishment meal."

"Holy smokes, Snort, that would be the worst thing you could do. That owl has soaked up all the deadly toxins. Eating her would be like eating a whole trainload of poison, train and all. Sudden death, that's what she is."

They whispered some more. Then Snort gave their reply. "Coyote brothers not believe stupid dummy ranch dog. Brothers not scared of poisum 'cause brothers make poisum with cannibal song, ho ho."

"And you think that makes you immune?"

He stared at me with his brutish yellow eyes. "Coyote not a mune. Coyote a cammible, and proudest of it to be."

I had to think fast. "Snort, we don't have time to argue. If you want to discuss this further, you can do it with the Wolf Creek Volunteer Poison Squad. They'll be here any minute, with men and trucks and gas masks."

That opened their eyes. "Uh. People coming?"

"Oh yes, hundreds of them. In fact . . . " I cocked my ear. "Yes, I think I hear their trucks this very minute."

They held another conference. "Rip and Snort still not believing dummy ranch dog, not hearing trucks coming and not scared of poisum."

It was looking bad. But just then the wind rustled in the cottonwood tree above us and—you won't believe this—five or six dead leaves floated down between us. No doubt they had been scorched by the terrible heat, but the ignoramuses didn't know that.

I pointed to the leaves. "Uh oh. You see? That tree just died from the poison, Snort, and with its last dying gasp, it has sent you a secret message."

The brothers scowled. "What secret message?"

"Don't you get it? Come on, Snort, wake up! I came to warn you and now the tree is warning you. It's telling you what to do. It's right here in front of your nose." I pointed my paw at one of the leaves on the ground. "What is that?"

"Leave." At first it didn't soak in, but then Snort's eyes popped open. "Leave?"

"Right, exactly. Noah, Lot, disaster, leave!"

They mumbled and muttered. Then, "Uh. Coyote know a lot, smell disaster and leave like tree."

They began backing away. Then they turned and vanished into the brush. Just before they left, I heard Snort mutter, "That pretty strong music for sure."

Silence. They were gone. I almost fainted with relief. Then I heard Madame's voice behind me.

"My goodness, unless my eyes deceive me, it's Hank the Rabbit."

"We've been through this before, Madame, and I don't have the energy to argue. Hank the Rabbit's okay with me. I feel like a rabbit right now."

"And you've sent the ruffians packing. I'm so proud! My goodness, they were going to eat me."

"I noticed. I also noticed that you were going to let them. What's the deal? "

"Well, as you can see, they bound me with grapevine, pinning my wings to my sides. And how can I do a proper job of casting spells without my wings? It can't be done. The wing is the sting. Disable the wing, dispose of the sting. Speaking of which . . . do you suppose you could unbind me. As it is, I'm bound to be tied."

"Well, I'll see what I can do."

I began gnawing on the grapevine. Whilst I was doing this, Madame kept me entertained with her chatter, such as:

"You're tickling me. Stop that. No, don't stop that. Continue. Oh, eee, ah! I suppose you know you are gnawing on my rib cage, and I suppose you gnaw, knowing full well what you're doing. Now I know you gnaw, trah-lah, trah-lah, trah-lah."

That was typical Madame Moonshine talk. She didn't always make sense but she seemed to enjoy herself. At last I cut her free. She smiled and flapped her wings.

"There! Thank you, thank you, and thank you. But how can I ever thank you enough? Thanks is such a paltry gift, but if I offered you a chicken instead, it would be a poultry gift. Hence, by following the logic of the moon and stars, we receive the knowledge that mere thanks is more thankful than a chicken."

"I guess so. Whatever."

She swiveled her head around and studied me with her big owlish eyes. "Do you suppose we can use that information, Hank the Rabbit?"

"Uh, Cowdog, actually. Hank the Cowdog."

"Oh rubbish. Cowdogness seems so boring and ordinary, but rabbitness has a way of keeping things hopping. And did I mention that you're spending the summer with me in my cave?"

"Huh? Spending the . . . no, we haven't discussed that . . . uh . . . yet . . . Madame."

"Oh piffle. I meant to tell you, but I was about to be eaten by cannibals and it slipped my mind. And besides, you just got here. Come, let's retire to my cave and we can discuss our summer plans."

She went hopping toward the bluffs on the other side of the creek. I followed . . . although I was beginning to feel a little uneasy about the summer business. When we came to the tree that was decorated by her bodyguard, Timothy the Turbo Windbag, she stopped.

"Timothy, you have been a naughty snake. How shameful and scandalous, allowing two ignoramus coyotes to tie you to a tree! I may be forced to review your employment record. It simply looks bad for a tree to be wearing my bodyguard. Come, Hank the Rabbit."

I followed her across the creek and to the bluffs. There, she disappeared into a hole and I followed. I crawled through the darkness for ten feet or so, until it opened up into a kind of underground room.

She stood beside a flat-topped rock in the middle, with tree roots hanging around her head. She was looking down at the flat-topped rock and . . . I didn't know what she was doing. Muttering, I suppose.

"Go left. Go right. Stand up. Sit down." She glanced up at me and smiled. "My troop of performing fleas. Would you like to say hello to them?"

"Uh . . . not really. Fleas and I don't get along. That is, we'll get along fine as long as they stay over there."

She clapped her wings together and turned her eyes on me. "Well, we are safe from marauding coyotes, and 'twas foolish of you to enter my cave, oh Rabbity Hank, because I just might not allow you to leave. But before I don't allow you to leave, tell me why you came."

"Well, Madame, I have a small problem."

"Oh good. A small problem is only half as large as a large one, so we needn't bother with it."

"Okay, I've got a large problem."

"Oh dear." She blinked her big moon eyes. "What have you done?"

I started at the beginning and told her the whole story about the grasshopper, the root stimulator, the mopwater, and the fight I'd picked with Billy's pet gorilla.

"See, I talked my way into a fight with one of the biggest, meanest dogs in Texas, and I don't know how to get out of it."

"Yes, it's coming clear. If you don't fight, you're a coward. If you do fight, you're a hamburger."

"Right, and I was hoping that you might be able to teach me some fighting tricks—you know, like karate or judo."

She rolled her eyes toward the ceiling. "Karate or judo, kersplotting menudo, we're plotting but you know—the answer is no." Her eyes drifted down to me. "I know many things about many things, little things about big things, and big things about little things. But I know no things about . . . fighting. In my line of work, we don't fight. We use our minds."

"Yeah, I saw you using your mind on those cannibals and it almost got you eaten."

"But I didn't need to use my mind. You used yours. One mind is enough, yours or mine, and I don't mind that it wasn't mine. The result was the same."

"We got lucky, Madame. That was pure-dee dumb blind-hog luck, and I'd just as soon have something more substantial when I go into battle with Rufus."

"Rufus. An interesting name. Does he say roof-roof?"

"That's probably the nicest thing he says."

"Hmmm." She raised a wing and began stroking some of the tree roots above her. "Rufus. Root stimulator. I am stimulating the roots on the roof of my cave. May I think about this?"

"Sure. Go ahead."

"Yes, we have the entire summer, don't we?"

"Well, I . . . to be honest, Madame, I really . . ."

"Hush. Silence."

She closed her eyes and went into a thinking spell. I could only hope that it was a good one.

12

CAUTION: SCARY ENDING

As the minutes dragged by, I began to suspect that Madame Moonshine wasn't thinking about my problem; she had totally checked out and gone to sleep. I got a clue from the fact that she snored.

"Madame? Madame Moonshine? I don't want to rush you, but I'm operating on a deadline. Madame, wake up."

Her eyes popped open. She stared at me and blinked. "You are in my cave."

"Yes ma'am, I realize that."

"Were you invited? And where is Timothy?"

"Yes, I was invited, and the last time we saw Tim, he was tied to a tree. The coyotes, remember?"

"Oh yes. It's coming back." She yawned. "And I have found the solution to your problem. It's so simple, I don't know why I didn't think of it sooner." She closed her eyes and raised her wings.

"The universe is composed of three basic elements: rock, paper, and scissors."

"I thought the elements were fire, water, and . . . something else. Mud? I don't remember."

"No. Rock, paper, and scissors. Rock is hard and can break scissors. Scissors are sharp and can cut paper. Paper is obscurative and can cover

rock. Which is the strongest of the three elements?"

"Well, I . . . I really don't know. But what does
this have to do with . . . "

"It has everything to do with everything, oh Rabbity Hank. It means that all things are strong, but
all things are weak. Rufus is a rock. If you are a scis-
sor, he will break you. So you must be . . . what?"

I puzzled over the answer. "A bigger rock? A
sludge hammer? I don't know, Madame."

Her eyes flew open. "Paper, you ninny. You
must attack him with your strength. Cover rock
with paper. Attack the large with the small."

And then she dropped her voice to a whisper
and told me the secret for winning the fight.

You'd probably like to know the secret, wouldn't
you? Ha, ha. Not yet. Be patient. We have to wait
and see if it worked.

My next problem was getting out of there.
Madame wanted to keep me for the rest of the
summer, if you recall, because she was getting
bored with her roots and snakes, I suppose. It
took me several minutes of hard talking to con-
vince her that I had a steady job and really
needed to be going.

She walked me to the mouth of the cave. "And I suppose this is goodbye, Rabbity Hank. Will you come see me again some time?"

"Sure, Madame, especially if your trick works and I survive the fight with Rufus. I'm still a little concerned about that."

"Oh piffle. Of course it will work. It's based upon universal principles. But just in case, I wish you luck."

"Thanks, Madame. See you around—I hope."

And with that, I left her there, waving her wing. I walked past the tree where . . . yikes, I almost walked into Big Tim. He had worked himself loose and was sulking in a big coil on the ground. I made a wide detour around him, set my course to the east, and headed down the creek.

I arrived at the appointed hill on time, and with a few minutes to spare. Plato and Beulah had been watching for me, and when they saw me on the hill, they came at a run.

Plato was the first to speak. "Hank, by golly, we weren't sure you'd make it, and to be honest, Beulah and I were hoping you wouldn't. It's just too risky, Hank. It's not worth it. We've put up with Rufus for a long time and surely we can stand it a while longer."

Beulah nodded. "Plato's right. It's not your problem, Hank, and if anything happened to you . . ."

"What Beulah's trying to say, if I may intrude here, is that we would be upset, Hank, very upset if . . . I mean, we appreciate your concern but . . . Hank, that dog is a killer. I know you're a pretty skilled fighter, but this guy is a professional thug. Call it off, Hank. Go home. Save yourself for another day."

Beulah nodded. "We'll understand."

I looked past them and saw . . . gulp . . . a huge Doberman pinscher coming up the hill. His little green eyes were sparkling and he wore a toothy smile.

"Sorry, but I started this thing and I've got to finish it."

Plato shook his head and walked a few steps away. "I knew it. Beulah, I told you he wouldn't listen to reason. Pride, that's what it is, just stubborn pride."

By that time I could hear Rufus's footsteps. Boom, boom, boom. I looked into Beulah's eyes. They were pleading and lovely and . . . and then Rufus stepped between us.

He pushed her out of the way. I swallowed down my fear and beamed him the sternest gaze I could come up with. "Rufus, I've already warned you about being rude to the ladies. I guess you didn't listen."

"Ha, ha, ha. I guess I didn't, bozo, and so what? I don't listen to you or anyone else." He squared his shoulders. "Are you sure you want this? 'Cause I ain't going to show any mercy."

"Good. Neither am I. Let's get started."

Plato and Beulah gasped and turned away. Rufus lowered himself into a crouch and began circling me. What did I do? I engaged the Madame Moonshine Strategy, and you're probably wondering what it was.

Heh, heh. It was very simple and very sneaky. Remember what she told me? "Attack the large with the small." Remember her trained fleas? Before I left her cave, she loaded them on my back, with orders for them to attack the nearest warm object when I gave the command word— "Tallyho!"

And that's just what I did. All at once my back came alive as two combat divisions of hungry fleas went on the attack. In a matter of seconds they had hopped to the ground and then onto Rufus.

He was still circling me, grinning, growling, sneering, glaring, and preparing to launch his first piledriver attack. Then, all at once, his eyes blanked out. He stopped, sat down, and began scratching his ear with a hind leg.

"Hey Rufus, what's the deal? I thought this was a fight."

"Shut up, moron, I've got to scratch. Don't leave." He scratched, stood up, and faced me again . . . then let out a squawl and started biting at a flea on his tail section. "I'll be with you in just a . . . gadzooks, these fleas are killin' me!"

"Hey Rufus, when you get tired of scratching fleas, let's talk. See, I'm the one who brought them, and I'm the only one who can call 'em off."

He snarled at me. "Why you . . . EEEE-YOW!" All at once he was spinning in circles. This must have gone on for several minutes. Beulah and Plato turned around and began watching. And then laughing.

At last Rufus had had enough. He had chased his tail so long and hard that he was worn out. "Okay, okay. Call 'em off, I give."

"Fleas, halt." The instant the fleas stopped biting, Rufus bared his fangs and jumped me—which gave me a little preview of how the fight would have gone without the fleas. In two seconds, he had me laid out on the ground and was sitting on me.

"Okay, smart guy, now you'll pay!" I saw his lips rise and his shark jaws open wide.

"Fleas, tallyho! Tallyho, and don't spare the horses!"

They must have stuck him pretty hard, because all at once he was rooting around in the dirt—chasing fleas and screaming for me to call them off.

I got up off the ground. "Fleas, halt!" They halted and Rufus stopped scratching. Panting for breath, he looked at me with weary eyes.

"Okay, cowdog, you win, but you had to cheat to do it."

"Call it what you will, Rufus, but the result is that you're going to be a better dog. See, I'm leaving the fleas with you. They're going to be your conscience. They have been programmed and trained to attack at the first sign of rude behavior. What do you think of that?"

"Oh swell. I always wanted to be," he curled his lip, "a good dog. What a drag."

"You'll get used to it, and when you do, the fleas will return to Madame Moonshine—who, by the way, was the brains behind this deal."

"I never heard of her, but if I ever get my paws on her, I'll . . . " The fleas stuck him. He gritted his teeth until they stopped biting. "I'll tell her . . . thank you."

"How sweet."

"Yeah. My ma would be proud, even if I ain't." He heaved a sigh and started walking back to Billy's house. "What a lousy punishment. I've got to be good for the rest of my life. I ain't sure I can stand myself."

When he was gone, I found myself looking into Beulah's adoring gaze. "Oh Hank!" She flew into the middle of me and engulferated me with hugs and kisses. "You were so noble and heroic! How can we ever repay you?"

I was about to suggest that she could start by ditching her bird dog boyfriend, but he was right there in my face, pumping my arm and slapping me on the back.

"By golly, Hank, what a triumph! Using trained fleas. Now, that was clever. Who would have thought of that? Nice work, by golly, nice work."

He shouldn't have done all that pumping and slapping. It must have jiggled my innards and stirred things up in my . . . there was Beulah, standing next to me, with the light of love shining in her eyes, within my grisp and grasp, and all I could think about was . . .

Burp.

I looked into her lovely face and saw . . . MOP-WATER. She had become a dirty mop and I couldn't stand the sight of her, and fellers, I was so sick I had to get out of there!

And now you know why The Mopwater Files must remain Top Secret, and why I can never tell this story to you or anyone else. It's just too sad and tragic.

Sorry. Case closed.

You can leave now. And don't drink any mop-water. I was sick for three days.

How can that bird dog be so lucky?

Have you read all of Hank's adventures?
Available in paperback at $6.95:

Also available on cassettes:
Hank the Cowdog's Greatest Hits!